ADA LIMÓN

IN
Praise
OF
Mystery

illustrated by
PETER SÍS

Norton Young Readers
An Imprint of W. W. Norton & Company
Independent Publishers Since 1923

For information about permission to reproduce selections from this book, write to
Permissions, W. W. Norton & Company, Inc., 500 Fifth Avenue, New York, NY 10110

For information about special discounts for bulk purchases, please contact
W. W. Norton Special Sales at specialsales@wwnorton.com or 800-233-4830

Manufacturing by Phœnix
Book design by Hana Anouk Nakamura
Production manager: Delaney Adams

ISBN 978-1-324-05400-9

W. W. Norton & Company, Inc., 500 Fifth Avenue, New York, N.Y. 10110
www.wwnorton.com

W. W. Norton & Company Ltd., 15 Carlisle Street, London W1D 3BS

1 2 3 4 5 6 7 8 9 0

Arching under the night sky inky
with black expansiveness, we point
to the planets we know,

we pin quick wishes on stars.

From earth, we read the sky
as if it is an unerring book
of the universe, expert
and evident.

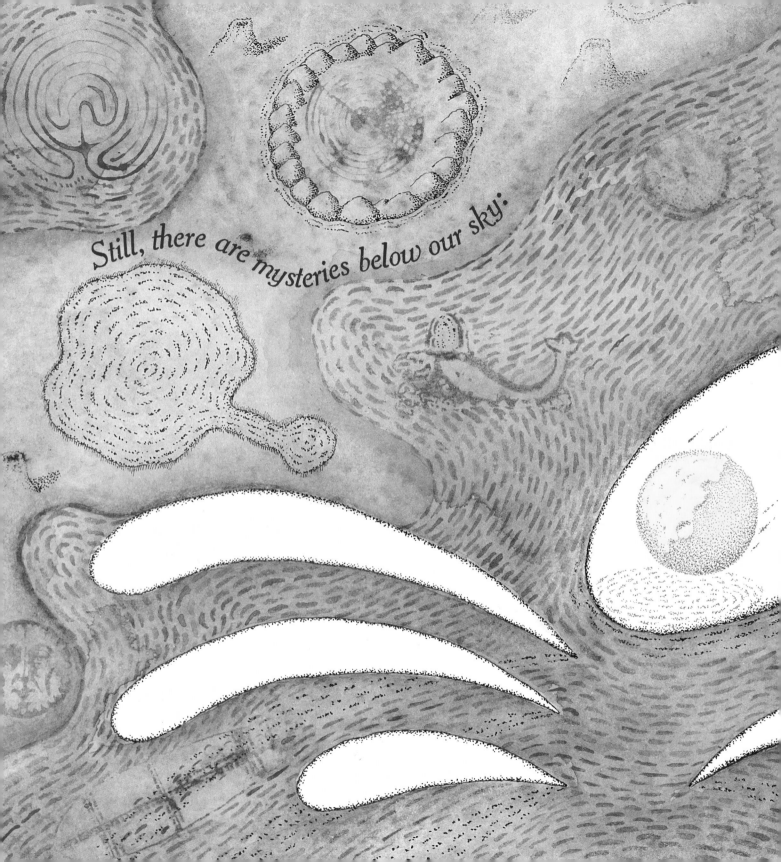

Still, there are mysteries below our sky:

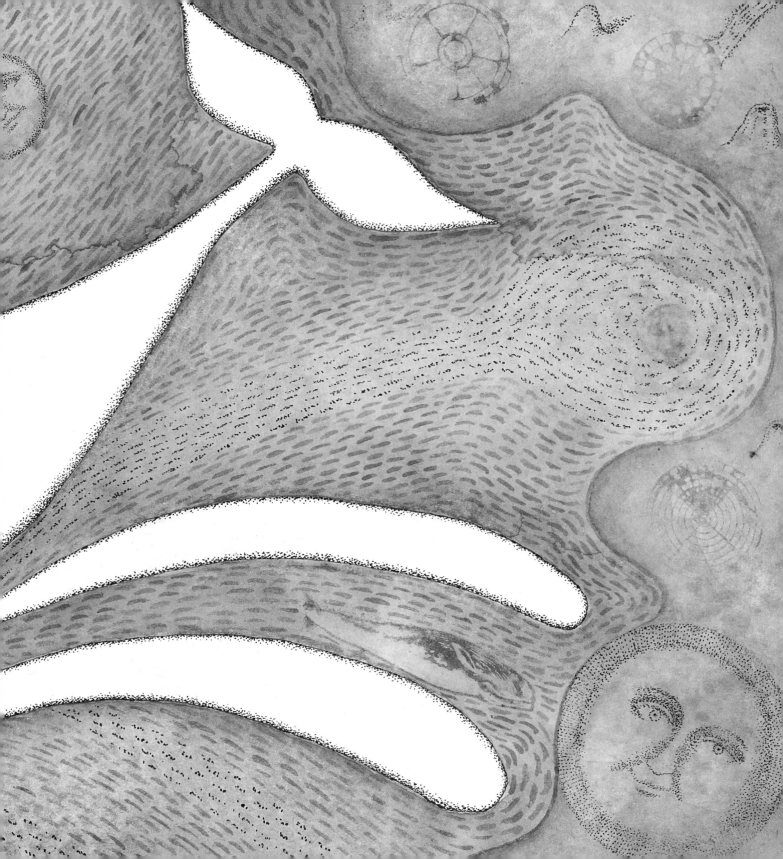

the whale song,

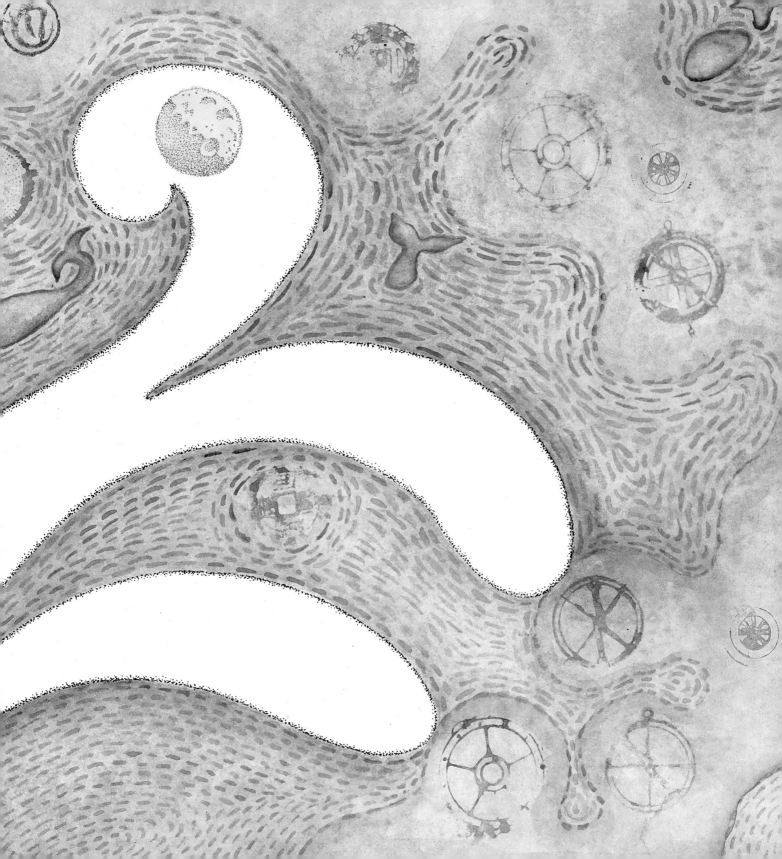

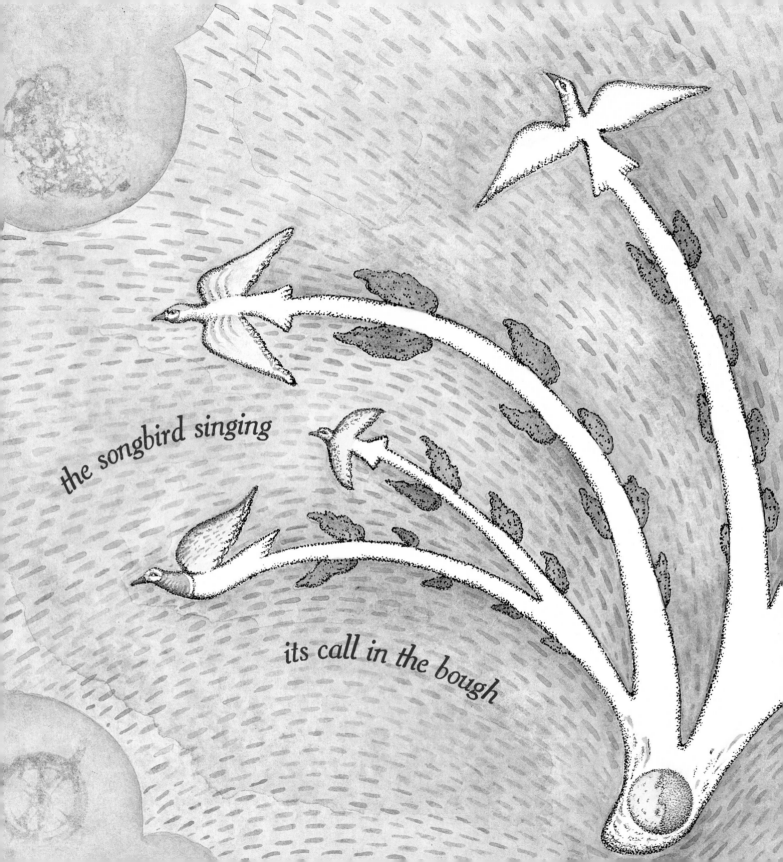

the songbird singing

its call in the bough

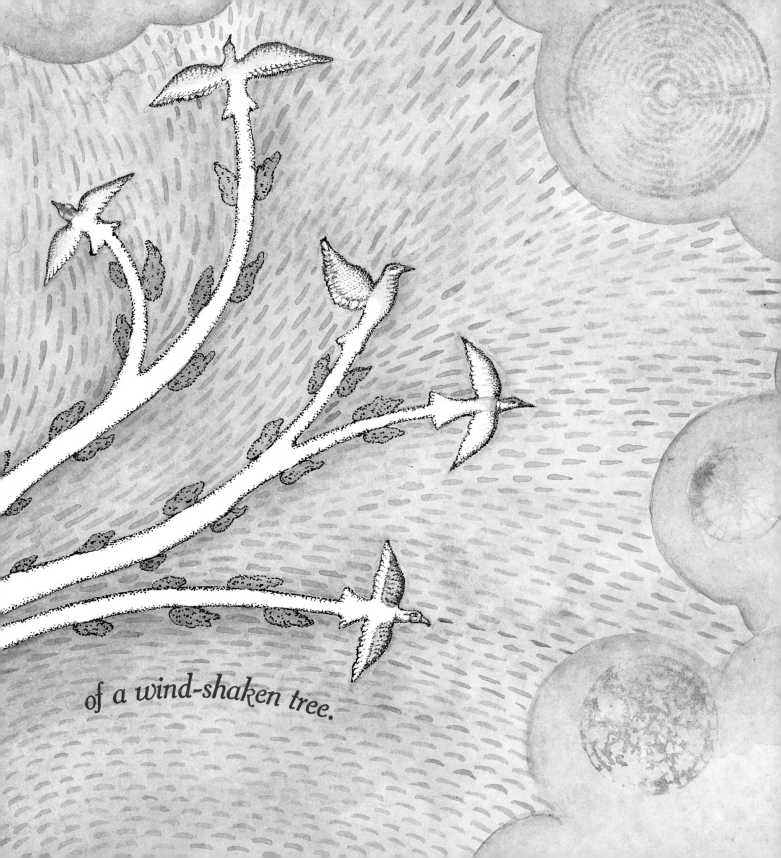

of a wind-shaken tree.

We are creatures of constant awe,
curious at beauty, at leaf and blossom,

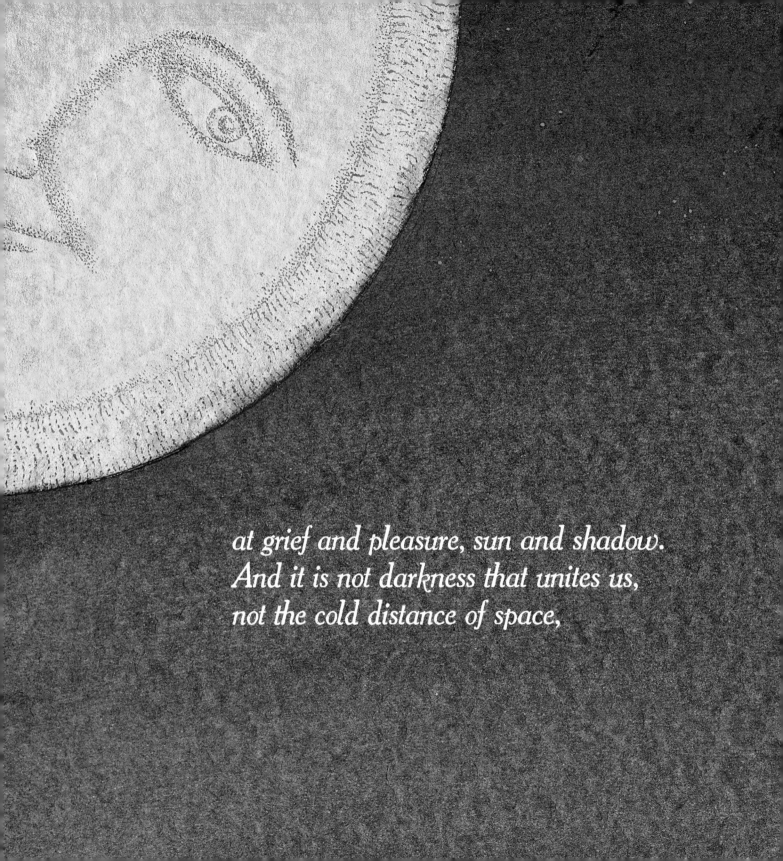

at grief and pleasure, sun and shadow.
And it is not darkness that unites us,
not the cold distance of space,

but the offering of water, each drop of rain,

each rivulet, each pulse, each vein.

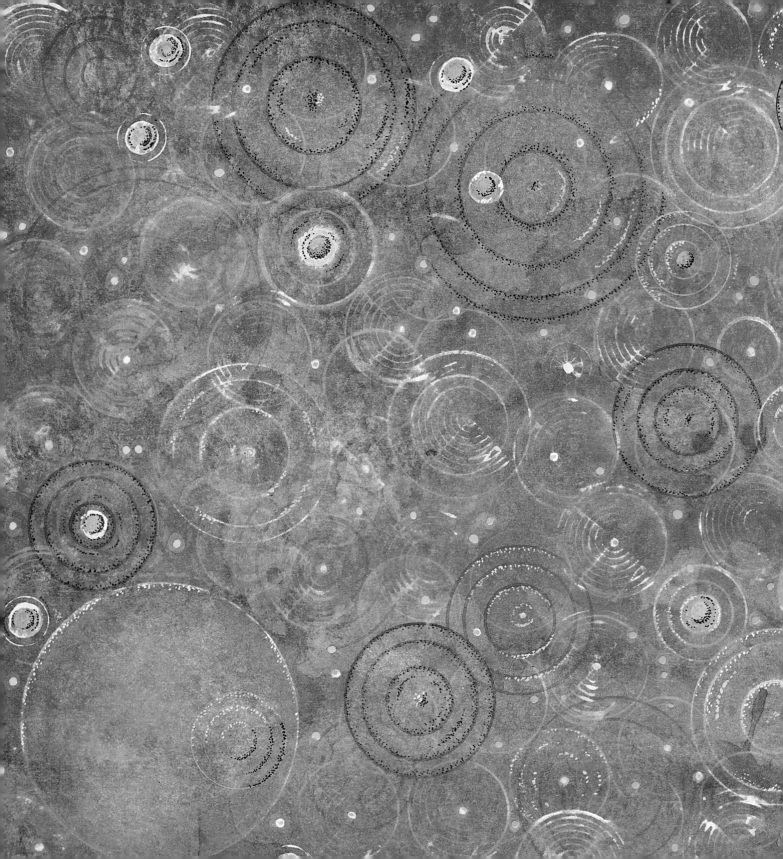

O second moon, we, too, are made

of water,

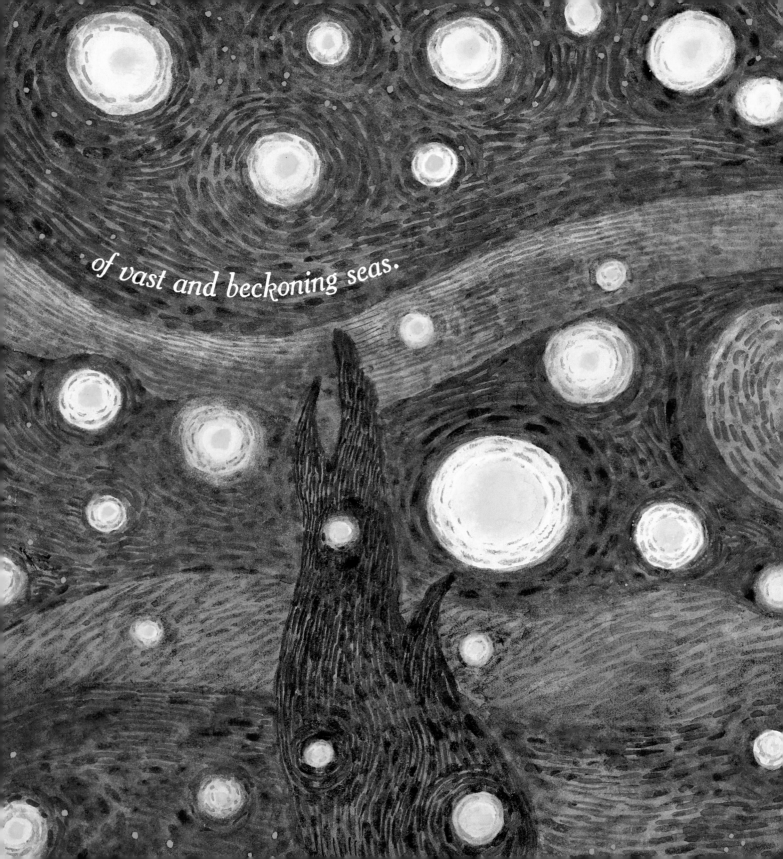

of vast and beckoning seas.

We, too, are made of wonders, of great
and ordinary loves,

of small invisible worlds,

of a need to call out through the dark.

In Praise of Mystery: A Poem for Europa

Arching under the night sky inky
with black expansiveness, we point
to the planets we know, we

pin quick wishes on stars. From earth,
we read the sky as if it is an unerring book
of the universe, expert and evident.

Still, there are mysteries below our sky:
the whale song, the songbird singing
its call in the bough of a wind-shaken tree.

We are creatures of constant awe,
curious at beauty, at leaf and blossom,
at grief and pleasure, sun and shadow.

And it is not darkness that unites us,
not the cold distance of space, but
the offering of water, each drop of rain,

each rivulet, each pulse, each vein.
O second moon, we, too, are made
of water, of vast and beckoning seas.

We, too, are made of wonders, of great
and ordinary loves, of small invisible worlds,
of a need to call out through the dark.

Author's Note

The poem "In Praise of Mystery" was written to make a journey beyond our planet. Engraved on NASA's *Europa Clipper* spacecraft, it will travel 1.8 billion miles from Earth to Jupiter's second moon, called Europa.

Like Earth, Europa is a water world: scientists believe that a vast ocean lies beneath its icy surface, holding more water than all Earth's oceans combined. Because water is one of the ingredients essential for life, Europa has always intrigued scientists. The *Europa Clipper* spacecraft will study Europa for signs that the chemistry and other conditions that could support life are present.

Europa Clipper is scheduled for launch in October 2024 and to enter Jupiter's orbit in 2030. For more information about the spacecraft and its mission, visit https://nasa.gov/europaclipper.

Even though the poem was meant to travel outward into space, I also wrote it to celebrate and honor the wonders of our own precious planet.

Ada Limón